Geronimo Stilton
ENGLISH!

20 I FEEL SICK! 我生病了！

U0061305

新雅文化事業有限公司

www.sunya.com.hk

Geronimo Stilton English
I FEEL SICK!　我生病了！

作　　者：Geronimo Stilton 謝利連摩・史提頓
譯　　者：申倩
責任編輯：王燕參
封面繪圖：Giuseppe Facciotto
插圖繪畫：Claudio Cernuschi, Andrea Denegri, Daria Cerchi
內文設計：Angela Ficarelli, Raffaella Picozzi
出　　版：新雅文化事業有限公司
　　　　　香港筲箕灣耀興道3號東匯廣場9樓
　　　　　營銷部電話：（852）2562 0161
　　　　　客戶服務部電話：（852）2976 6559
　　　　　傳真：（852）2597 4003
　　　　　網址：http://www.sunya.com.hk
　　　　　電郵：marketing@sunya.com.hk
發　　行：香港聯合書刊物流有限公司
　　　　　香港新界大埔汀麗路36號中華商務印刷大廈3字樓
　　　　　電話：（852）2150 2100　傳真：（852）2407 3062
　　　　　電郵：info@suplogistics.com.hk
印　　刷：C & C Offset Printing Co.,Ltd
　　　　　香港新界大埔汀麗路36號
版　　次：二〇一二年二月初版
　　　　　10 9 8 7 6 5 4 3 2 1

ISBN: 978-962-08-5490-3
© 2008 Edizioni Piemme S.p.A., Via Tiziano 32 - 20145 Milano - Italia
International Rights © 2007 Atlantyca S.p.A. - via Leopardi, 8, Milano - Italy
© 2012 for this Work in Traditional Chinese language, Sun Ya Publications (HK) Ltd.
9/F, Eastern Central Plaza, 3 Yiu Hing Rd, Shau Kei Wan, Hong Kong
Published and printed in Hong Kong

CONTENTS
目錄

BENJAMIN'S CLASSMATES
班哲文的老師和同學們

Maestra Topitilla
托比蒂拉·德·托比莉斯

Rarin
拉琳

Diego
迪哥

Rupa
露芭

Tui
杜爾

David
大衛

Sakura
櫻花

Mohamed
穆哈麥德

Tian Kai
田凱

Oliver
奧利佛

Milenko
米蘭哥

Trippo
特里普

Carmen
卡敏

Atina
阿提娜

Esmeralda
愛絲梅拉達

Pandora
潘朵拉

Takeshi
北野

Kuti
菊花

Benjamin
班哲文

Hsing
阿星

Laura
羅拉

Kiku
奇哥

Antonia
安東妮婭

Liza
麗莎

GERONIMO AND HIS FRIENDS
謝利連摩和他的家鼠朋友們

謝利連摩・史提頓 Geronimo Stilton
一個古怪的傢伙，簡直可以說是一隻笨拙的文化鼠。他是《鼠民公報》的總裁，正花盡心思改變報紙業的歷史。

菲・史提頓 Tea Stilton
謝利連摩的妹妹，她是《鼠民公報》的特派記者，同時也是一個運動愛好者。

班哲文・史提頓 Benjamin Stilton
謝利連摩的小侄兒，常被叔叔稱作「我的小乳酪」，是一隻感情豐富的小老鼠。

潘朵拉・華之鼠 Pandora Woz
柏蒂・活力鼠的姨甥女、班哲文最好的朋友，是一隻活潑開朗的小老鼠。

柏蒂・活力鼠 Patty Spring
美麗迷人的電視新聞工作者，致力於她熱愛的電視事業。

賴皮 Trappola
謝利連摩的表弟，非常喜歡食物，風趣幽默，是一隻饞嘴、愛開玩笑的老鼠，善於將歡樂傳遞給每一隻鼠。

麗萍姑媽 Zia Lippa
謝利連摩的姑媽，對鼠十分友善，又和藹可親，只想將最好的給身邊的鼠。

艾拿 Iena
謝利連摩的好朋友，充滿活力，熱愛各項運動，他希望能把對運動的熱誠傳給謝利連摩。

史奎克・愛管閒事鼠 Ficcanaso Squitt
謝利連摩的好朋友，是一個非常有頭腦的私家偵探，總是穿着一件黃色的乾濕樓。

I'M FEELING FINE!
我覺得很好！

親愛的小朋友，你們好嗎？很好，真的嗎？我今天也覺得很好……不過其實昨天我懷疑自己患了流行性感冒而去了看醫生。嗯，是的，我就是這樣，有點膽小，只要感到有一點發冷頭暈就立刻跑去看醫生！昨天是這樣的：我感到喉嚨有點痛、頭有點痛、肚子也痛，而且全身都不舒服！你們想知道後來我怎樣了嗎？我這就告訴你們……當然是用英語說啦！

> *I'm feeling fine today!*

> *I'm feeling fine, too!*

I'm feeling fine.
我覺得很好！
I'm not feeling well.
我覺得不舒服！
I've got flu.
我患了流行性感冒。

I'm not feeling very well, perhaps I've got flu!

Uncle Geronimo, you must go to the doctor!

跟我謝利連摩 · 史提頓一起學英文，就像玩遊戲一樣簡單好玩！

你可以一邊看着圖畫一邊讀。
以下有幾個標誌，你要特別留意：

當看到 💿 標誌時，你可以聽CD，一邊聽，一邊跟着朗讀，還可以跟着一起唱歌。

當看到 ⭐ 標誌時，你可以和朋友們一起玩遊戲，或者嘗試回答問題。題目很簡單，它們對鞏固你所學過的內容很有幫助。

當看到 ❗ 標誌時，你要注意看一下格子裏的生字，反覆唸幾遍，掌握發音。

最後，不要忘記完成小測驗和練習冊裏的問題！看看你有多聰明吧。

祝大家學得開開心心！

謝利連摩 · 史提頓

AT THE CLINIC 在診所裏

我以一千塊莫澤雷勒乳酪發誓，我跟李克·斯蒂頓特醫生非常熟絡！他為我做了詳細的檢查後，對我說：「你沒有染上流行性感冒，只是有點累了！」

clinic 診所
waiting room 候診室
doctor 醫生
patient 病人
nurse 護士
checkup 檢查
prescription 藥方
stethoscope 聽診器

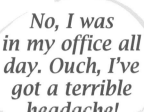

The doctor prescribes vitamins for Geronimo. He will be better soon!

A SONG FOR YOU!

Track 1

The Nice Doctor

When I am not feeling well,
I go to my friend the doctor.
He's nice,
He gives me sweets!

I go to my friend the doctor.
I listen to his advice,
take my medicine,
have a little rest
and enjoy my friends' company!
I go to my friend the doctor.

a bit 有點 / 有些

AT THE PHARMACY
在藥房裏

離開診所後，我拿着醫生開給我的藥方去藥房買一些維他命，順便買點其他東西，例如藥水膠布、消毒劑、牙刷、牙膏、漱口水等，我要補充的東西還真不少呢！

pharmacy　藥房	pills　藥丸
pharmacist　藥劑師	plasters　藥水膠布
counter　櫃台	disinfectant　消毒劑
shelves　貨架	mouthwash　漱口水
medicines　藥	toothbrush　牙刷
ointment　藥膏	dental floss　牙線
cough mixture　止咳藥	toothpaste　牙膏

11

AT THE DENTIST'S
在牙科診所裏

回家後，班哲文告訴我他感到牙痛，於是我陪他去看牙醫。在輪候時，班哲文看見診所內有很多不同的物品，便問我這些物品用英語該怎麼說，你也跟着他一起學習吧。

dental clinic 牙科診所	anaesthetic 麻醉藥
dentist 牙醫	dentist's chair 牙醫專用椅
assistant 助手	drill 鑽機
teeth 牙齒	pliers 鉗子
ache / pain 痛	dentist's mirror 牙醫專用鏡子
toothache 牙痛	cavity 牙齒蛀洞
anaesthesia 麻醉	filling 填滿

Dentist: Sit down, Benjamin, I'll check your teeth.
Benjamin: Yes, this tooth hurts a bit!

Dentist: Let me see. Open your mouth! Let's check that tooth!

★ 試着用英語說出以下詞彙：牙科診所、牙醫、牙痛。

答案：*dental clinic, dentist, toothache*

Dentist: Does it hurt here?
Benjamin: Ouch!
Dentist: You've got a little hole in your tooth. It's called "a cavity". It's not serious, but we had better fill it.

Benjamin: It won't hurt, will it?
Dentist: No, don't worry! Do you always brush your teeth with a toothbrush and floss them after meals?

接着，牙醫開始替班哲文補牙。

Dentist: You always have to brush your teeth after meals!

Don't worry, I'll take care of it!

Ok, you can go now!

It didn't hurt at all. Thanks!

We had better...
我們最好……

73

AT THE HOSPITAL
在醫院裏

賴皮總是喜歡捉弄我，但這次他不是開玩笑，他的腳真的很痛！於是菲把他送到醫院去看醫生，我急急趕到醫院去看他。

hospital 醫院
emergency
　department 急症室
ambulance 救護車
wheel chair 輪椅
crutches 拐杖
ground floor 地面
ward 病房
department 部門
injury 受傷

Where is Trappola? — He's at the emergency department.

Do we have to take the lift?

No, it's on the ground floor.

Hi Trappola, how are you?

My foot hurts and it's very swollen.

Number 107...

I was running and I... fell down!

It's your turn. I'll come with you!

It's almost certainly broken. You must have an X-ray at once!

I can see it's broken from the X-ray. We'll put your ankle in plaster.

For three weeks. Once you take it off, you'll have to do some exercises.

How long will I have to keep the plaster on for?

! have an X-ray
照X光

Thank you, doctor!

Oh... I understand!

⭐ 試着用英語説出:「我的腳受了傷,而且腫得很厲害。」

答案: My foot hurts and it's very swollen.

HI, HOW ARE YOU?
嗨，你覺得怎麼樣？

潘朵拉患了流行性感冒，沒有上學，於是班哲文一放學就趕去她家裏探望她⋯⋯
他倆真是最要好的朋友啊！

I've got a temperature.　　我發燒了。

I'M FEELING BETTER!
我覺得好些了！

這個星期天，大家又一起聚在我的家裏。我很高興見到大家都恢復了健康！

You are as fit as a fiddle!
你的身體狀況很好！

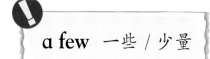

a few 一些／少量

And how about you, Trappola?

Then they took it off. I've exercised with my physiotherapist for a few days and... I'm fine now!

I kept my ankle in plaster for three weeks.

Yes, you look great, Trappola!

A SONG FOR YOU!

Track 2

I Feel Sick

I feel weak
I have a headache
I have a temperature
I have a stomachache!

It's troublesome to be sick,
but the doctor
will take care of me
and my mum will cuddle me.

Don't be afraid of the doctor,
he'll take care of you
and so you will be able
to play with your friends again!

It's troublesome to be sick,
but the doctor
will take care of me
and my mum will cuddle me!
I feel sick, I feel sick!

〈一場嚴重的感冒〉

菲：嗨，謝利連摩，你感冒好些了嗎？

謝利連摩：乞——乞嗤！！！

菲：看來你的病情比之前嚴重了。

菲：或許你應該留在家中多休息幾天。
謝利連摩：你是開玩笑吧？難道我要把這裏所有的工作都帶回家去？這不可能！

班哲文：嗨，叔叔，你覺得怎麼樣？
謝利連摩：不用擔心，班哲文，我沒事！

班哲文：乞——乞嗤！！！
菲：你還有什麼好説？
謝利連摩：這不能證明什麼！只是巧合而已！

馬克思爺爺：謝利連摩，你臉色很蒼白，讓我看看你有沒有發燒吧！
謝利連摩：啊？

Go home now! You're infecting the whole office!

I feel terribly guilty!

Don't worry, boss! Check this news from Topikistan!

But your...

馬克思爺爺：馬上回家去！你在這裏會傳染大家的！

謝利連摩：我感到非常內疚！

史丹塔：不用擔心，老闆！看看這個由老鼠克斯坦來的消息吧。
謝利連摩：但是你的……

... face is all red!

謝利連摩：……臉很紅！

Geronimo, look, I have goose pimples despite the heating!

You've all caught flu and it's my fault. I'm going home!

賴皮：謝利連摩，看，儘管已開了暖氣，我還是長滿了雞皮疙瘩。
謝利連摩：你們都患了流行性感冒，這都是我的錯。我現在就回家去！

I'm staying off for the rest of the week. I don't want everybody in the office to get ill... who will work on the paper otherwise?

謝利連摩：這星期裏餘下的幾天，我都會留在家中。我不想辦公室裏所有鼠都因我而染病……否則誰還能做這期報紙呢？

Has he gone?

Yes, you can come out!

菲：他走了嗎？
賴皮：走了，你可以出來了！

Fard?

Yes!

Hurry up, or Geronimo will get there before us!

How did you manage to get goose pimples?

I've put some hair gel on!

菲：這是胭脂？
史丹塔：對呀！
馬克思爺爺：快點兒，不然謝利連摩會比我們先到達那裏的！
潘朵拉：你是怎樣假扮長了雞皮疙瘩的？
賴皮：我在手臂上塗了一些髮膠。

Now, a nice cup of tea, a hot-water bottle, a nap...

謝利連摩：現在，我要來一杯茶，一個熱水瓶，小睡片刻……

It's party time!

Geronimo, this is our present...

... for the prize you've just won for your new book!

You were pretending, then!

Congratulations!

The End

菲：派對時間到了！
馬克思爺爺：謝利連摩，這是我們送給你的禮物……

賴皮：為了慶祝你的新書獲獎。
班哲文、潘朵拉、史丹塔：恭喜你！
謝利連摩：原來你們是假裝的！

TEST 小測驗

⭐ 1. 用英語說出下面的句子。

(a) 今天我覺得很好！I'm ... ...！

(b) 我也覺得很好！I'm ... ... , ...！

(c) 我覺得不舒服！I'm not ... ...！

(d) 你應該去看醫生！You must ... ...！

⭐ 2. 讀出下面的詞彙，並用中文說出它們的意思。

(a) nurse　　**(b) clinic**　　**(c) waiting room**　　**(d) patient**

⭐ 3. 謝利連摩對醫生說：「我的喉嚨很痛。」這句話用英語該怎麼說？圈出相應的英文句子。

I've got a terrible headache.

I've got a sore throat.

⭐ 4. 看看下面兩段對話，根據中文句子的意思，把英文句子說完整。

(a) 牙醫：你有沒有經常在進食後用牙刷刷牙？

班哲文：沒有經常這樣做。

牙醫：你應該經常在進食後刷牙。

Dentist: Do you always ... ... with a ... after meals?

Benjamin: Not ... .

Dentist: You always have to ... ... after meals.

(b) 班哲文：嗨，你覺得怎麼樣？

潘朵拉：我發燒了。

Hi, how ... you?

I've ... ...

DICTIONARY 詞典

A

a bit　有點 / 有些

ache　痛

advice　勸告

always　經常

ambulance　救護車

anaesthetic　麻醉藥

anaesthesia　麻醉

ankle　足踝

assistant　助手

B

breath　呼吸

brush　刷

C

cavity　牙齒蛀洞

checkup　檢查

clinic　診所

coincidence　巧合

cold　感冒

cough　咳嗽

cough mixture　止咳藥

counter　櫃台

crutches　拐杖

cuddle　擁抱

D

deep　深

dental clinic　牙科診所

dental floss　牙線

dentist　牙醫

dentist's chair　牙醫專用椅

dentist's mirror　牙醫專用鏡子

department　部門

disinfectant　消毒劑

doctor　醫生

drill 鑽機

E

emergency department
　急症室（普：急診室）

exercises 運動

F

face 臉

fard 胭脂

filling 填滿

flu 流行性感冒

foot 腳

friend 朋友

G

goose pimples 雞皮疙瘩

ground floor 地面

guilty 內疚

H

headache 頭痛

hospital 醫院

hurts 受傷

I

infecting 傳染

injury 受傷

K

kidding 開玩笑

L

lift 升降機

long 長

luckily 幸運地

M

medicine 藥

mouth 嘴巴

mouthwash 漱口水

must 必須

N

nap　小睡

news　消息

nose　鼻子

nurse　護士

O

office　辦公室

ointment　藥膏

P

pain　痛

patient　病人

perhaps　或許 / 也許

pharmacist　藥劑師

pharmacy　藥房

photo album　相簿

physiotherapist　物理治療師

pills　藥丸

plasters　藥水膠布 / 石膏

pliers　鉗子

prescribe　處方

prescription　藥方

present　禮物

pretending　假裝

prove　證明

R

recovered　康復

remember　記得

rest　休息

S

serious　嚴重

shelves　貨架

sick　生病

sit down　坐下

sore throat　喉嚨痛

stethoscope　聽診器

stomachache　肚子痛

sweets　糖果

swollen　腫起來

T

teeth　牙齒

temperature　發燒

terrible　極度

tired　疲倦

today　今天

tomorrow　明天

toothache　牙痛

toothbrush　牙刷

toothpaste　牙膏

troublesome　令人煩惱

U

understand　明白

V

vitamins　維他命

W

wait　等候

waiting room　候診室

ward　病房

weeks　星期

wheel chair　輪椅

worry　擔心

X

X-ray　X光

Y

yesterday　昨天

看在一千塊莫澤雷勒乳酪的份上，你學得開心嗎？很開心，對不對？好極了！跟你一起跳舞唱歌我也很開心！我等着你下次繼續跟班哲文和潘朵拉一起玩一起學英語呀。現在要說再見了，當然是用英語說啦！

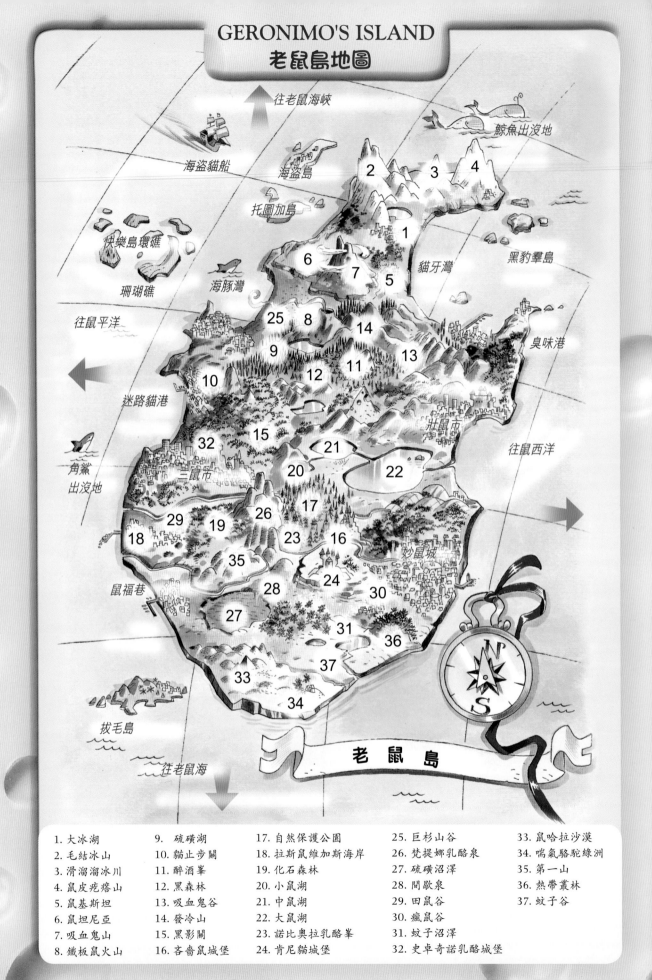

GERONIMO'S ISLAND
老鼠島地圖

往老鼠海峽

鯨魚出沒地

海盜貓船

海盜島

托圖加島

快樂島環礁

珊瑚礁

海豚灣

往鼠平洋

貓牙灣

黑豹羣島

臭味港

往鼠西洋

壯鼠市

迷路貓港

角鯊
出沒地

三鼠市

妙鼠城

鼠福巷

拔毛島

往老鼠海

老 鼠 島

Geronimo Stilton

EXERCISE BOOK
練習冊

想知道自己對 I FEEL SICK! 掌握了多少，
趕快打開後面的練習完成它吧！

ENGLISH!

20 **I FEEL SICK!** 我生病了！

I'M FEELING FINE!
我覺得很好！

⭐ 他們在說什麼？根據圖畫，選出適當的詞彙填在橫線上，完成他們的對話。

flu	feeling	doctor	well	fine

1. I'm _____ fine today!

2. I'm feeling _____, too!

3. I'm not feeling very _____, perhaps I've got _____!

4. Uncle Geronimo, you must go to the _____!

AT THE CLINIC 在診所裏

⭐ 謝利連摩去診所看病。根據圖畫，選出正確的詞彙填在橫線上。

> nurse　　patient　　doctor　　stethoscope

1. _____

2. _____

3. _____

4. _____

AT THE PHARMACY
在藥房裏

⭐ 謝利連摩到藥房去買東西，看看他買了些什麼，根據圖畫，在橫線上填寫缺少的英文字母，你就知道了。你還可以給圖畫填上顏色呢。

1. __ i n t __ e n t

2. t o __ t h p __ s t e

3. t o o __ h b r __ s h

4. __ i l __ s

5. p l __ s t e __ s

AT THE DENTIST'S
在牙科診所裏

⭐ 班哲文去看牙醫。根據圖畫，選出適當的詞彙填在橫線上，完成他們的對話。

teeth	down	hurt	cavity
mouth	check	hole	

1. Sit _____ ,
Benjamin, I'll check
your _____ .

2. Let me see.
Open your _____ !
Let's _____
that tooth!

3. Does it
_____ here?

Ouch!

4. You've got
a little _____
in your tooth.
It's called "a
_____ ".

AT THE HOSPITAL
在醫院裏

⭐ 賴皮的腳受了傷，謝利連摩和菲帶他去醫院看病。你知道下面這些與醫院有關的英文詞彙的意思嗎？把相配的中英文詞彙用線連起來。

1. hospital　●　　　●　急症室

2. ambulance　●　　　●　發燒

3. checkup　●　　　●　檢查

4. wheel chair　●　　　●　醫院

5. ward　●　　　●　受傷

6. temperature　●　　　●　輪椅

7. injury　●　　　●　病房

8. emergency department　●　　　●　救護車

HI, HOW ARE YOU?
嗨，你覺得怎麼樣？

⭐ 潘朵拉病了，班哲文去探望她。從下面選出適當的詞彙填在橫線上，完成他們的對話。（每個選項只可使用一次）

> luckily   temperature   cough   nose
> you   cold   anything   medicine

1. Hi, Pandora, how are _____ ?

2. I've got a _____ .

3. Have you caught a _____, too?

4. Yes, I keep blowing my _____ .

5. Have you got a _____ ?

6. No, no cough, _____ !

7. Did you take _____ ?

8. Yes, I took the _____ the doctor prescribed.

I'M FEELING BETTER!
我覺得好些了！

★ 謝利連摩、賴皮和班哲文的病都好了。看看他們在跟柏蒂説些什麼，選出適當的句子填在橫線上，完成他們的對話。

> I'm fine.   Then they took it off.
> I feel sick.   No more toothache!

Ger: I went to the doctor because (1) _____

_____

But now (2) _____

Ben: I had to have a filling but I'm fine now.

(3) _____

Trap: I kept my ankle in plaster for three weeks.

(4) _____

ANSWERS　答案

TEST　小測驗

1. (a) I'm <u>feeling</u> <u>fine</u> <u>today</u>!　　(b) I'm <u>feeling</u> <u>fine, too</u>!

　(c) I'm not <u>feeling</u> <u>very</u> <u>well</u>!　　(d) You must <u>go</u> <u>to</u> <u>the</u> <u>doctor</u>!

2. (a) 護士　　(b) 診所　　(c) 候診室　　(d) 病人

3. I've got a sore throat.

4. (a) Dentist: Do you always <u>brush</u> <u>your</u> <u>teeth</u> with a <u>toothbrush</u> after meals?

　　Benjamin: Not <u>always</u>.

　　Dentist: You always have to <u>brush</u> <u>your</u> <u>teeth</u> after meals.

　(b) Hi, how <u>are</u> you?

　　I've <u>got</u> <u>a</u> <u>temperature</u>.

EXERCISE BOOK　練習冊

P.1

1. feeling　　2. fine　　3. well, flu　　4. doctor

P.2

1. stethoscope　　2. nurse　　3. doctor　　4. patient

P.3

1. <u>o</u>int<u>m</u>ent　　2. to<u>o</u>thp<u>a</u>ste　　3. too<u>t</u>hb<u>r</u>ush　　4. p<u>i</u>lls　　5. pl<u>a</u>ster<u>s</u>

P.4

1. down, teeth　　2. mouth, check　　3. hurt　　4. hole, cavity

P.5

1. hospital 醫院　　2. ambulance 救護車　　3. checkup 檢查

4. wheel chair 輪椅　　5. ward 病房　　6. temperature 發燒

7. injury 受傷　　8. emergency department 急症室

P.6

1. you　2. temperature　3. cold　4. nose　5. cough　6. luckily　7. anything　8. medicine

P.7

1. I feel sick.　　2. I'm fine.　　3. No more toothache!　　4. Then they took it off.